A OUT OF THE BLU

A SULTY INK SERIES

A Novel By,

SONJA B.

Contains explicit language & adult themes suitable for ages 17+

Your FACE you would

Look better BETWEEN our pages!

Check us out at

www.afterhourspublications.com

Chapter 1

"Dad! Dad!" I call out to my father who is covered in blood of the attacker who just killed my mom. Dad slowly turned around, the color of his eyes is no longer the deep brown they normally are but an electric blue with hints of gold speckling his irises. His body has expanded with hair that has sprouted out along his hands, face, and neck. His teeth have elongated with fang-like canines. He looked like he was fighting an internal battle within himself. He stares at me with so much intent and lets out a painful howl.

I wake sitting straight up in my bed covered in sweat and shaking. It has been 15 years since that dreadful night, when my mother was murdered, and I found out who my family really was. My father never was the same after her death, but he made sure I learned who and what I am. That night I found out that my family are wolf shifters. Not like the kind you see on TV where someone is bit by a wolf, we were true blood werewolves, descendants from a pack in Africa. My mother, the daughter of the Alpha to the Adeyemi Pack, was supposed to be mated to the son of the Alpha of the Okoye Pack. Unfortunately, he was not her true mate. My father was. My father was one of my grandfather's guards. From the beginning, they knew that they were true mates. She tried to explain this to my grandfather, but he would not listen and only saw the greater power of merging the two packs. After plotting and planning, my mother and father finally escaped the pack to America.

They never remained too long in one city to put down roots. They didn't know if her father or the other Alpha's son was still looking for them. After three years of no one popping up, and with my mother becoming pregnant with me, they decided to settle in Texarkana, Texas, a place that was up and coming and had enough woods for them to hunt and relax in their true form.

Things were going good for them for a while. My father was a police detective, and my mother was a Principal at one of the local high schools. Life was pretty awesome. My parents doted on me and made sure I never wanted for anything. When I was eleven, we went on our annual camping trip. Not knowing that we were on another packs land, they attacked my mom and killed her. That was the night I found out who and what my family was. My father told me what happened with my grandfather and them escaping to America. He also told me that someday my grandfather or the other alpha still might show, so I had to be very aware of the people I let in my life. After that, my dad started training me in combat and weaponry. One day I was so tired and exhausted from training so hard that I asked him,

"Dad, why do I have to learn all this stuff? We are in America. It's not like we live in a war-torn country."

He took a deep breath and pulled me into hug and said, "Blu, I never want you to be in a situation where you couldn't protect yourself." So, learning boxing, martial arts, how to shoot damn near every gun known to man, and how to use a knife was my hardcore training every day with him till four years ago when dad was shot and killed on a bust that went bad. I think his death was the hardest because he was the only real family I had left.

Chapter 2

Mondays have never been my favorite day, but owning your own business has its perks of going in late. But this particular Monday is not the day. I have a 9am tattoo consult coming in. Did I not mention, I owned a tattoo shop? Yeah, that's my pride and joy. Sultry Ink has been in business for five years now and is growing bigger than any of the naysayers ever expected. My

father was my biggest supporter and always told me how proud he was of me. I got a crew of three workers that are more like family than employees. Hoss, my right hand, has been here with me since the beginning. He's more like a big brother than an employee. We met in high school and just clicked. Dad took him under his wing since he was an only child of a divorced mother and was constantly getting in trouble. Hence the reason, why he thinks he's somebody's big brother. Hell, we are only five months apart. Plus, he's a shifter too, a panther, so that helped.

My other two employees are Rocket and Pix. They're shifters too. Both have been with me since the beginning, and I wouldn't trade them for the world. Rocket, who is an eagle shifter, is an amazing tattoo artist and a male hoe. Lord knows how many chicks I've had to kick out of my shop bringing drama because of this man. Awesome artist, though. Now Pix, my foxy little fox shifter, is the shops receptionist and totally in a class of her own. Quiet, mousey, but let me tell you please, please, don't make her mad. A few of Rocket's fans found out the hard way. She's definitely silent but deadly. Yeah, we're a rag-tag bunch and nothing could make us any closer. *My family.*

Rolling out of the bed, I head to the bathroom to take a shower and handle my hygiene. Getting out of the shower, I wrap my shoulder length dreads in a towel and another around my body.

"What to wear today?" I ask myself as I stroll into my walk-in closet.

It's a sea of white, black, and grey. It makes getting dressed simple. I chose a pair of black ripped jeans, a Bob Marley tank, and a pair of Doc Marten boots. See, simple. As I'm getting ready, Bullet, my Great Dane, comes barging in.

I bend down to rub him behind his ears and say to him, "Hey boy! Damn Bullet you need a milk bone, your breath is ripe this morning. Are you ready to be let out, boy?"

He lets out a loud bark. I lead him out of my room, down the stairs to the kitchen, and let him out the back door. I take a second to take in the view of my backyard. This is the land and house that my parents bought when they moved here. I would never sell it. too many good memories, plus sometimes I can still feel they're presence here with me. My four-bedroom, three-bathroom, two-level brick house sits on 30 acres with a lake on it. There's enough room for me to let my wolf out without anyone seeing her. It's my own little piece of Heaven.

Returning to my room, I finish getting ready. As I stand in front of my full-length mirror, I take a good look at myself. I can see in my features what I have inherited from my parents. I have my mom's height, standing at 5'7" with a feminine toned shape. My Dad was 6'3". My tawny skin I got from them both, but my light hazel eyes I got from my Dad. Now dressed, I apply a minimal amount of make up with clear lip gloss. Love the natural look. I remove the towel from dreads and let them hang free.

Heading back downstairs to the kitchen, I grab my purse and head out to my all black Ford Excursion. Yeah, I drive a big-ass SUV, let me show you why..... I let out a loud whistle, "Bullet, here boy", I call out to my Great Dane, who comes barreling over hill towards me. Thank God for my werewolf strength because he would have knocked me over. I open the back door and he jumps in. I had the back seats and third row removed so I would have enough room for my supplies and his big ass.

The ride to town was smooth. Thank God it's only 30 minutes away. Feeling generous this morning, I pull into the local bakery to pick up doughnuts and coffee for the crew. Attaching Bullet's leash to his collar, we make our way inside. Hell yeah, he's going in there with me. Where I go, he goes. Thank God it's not busy this morning, I think to myself as I make my way to counter to place my order with Mrs. Jenkins, the town's gossip.

"Morning Mrs. Jenkins, can I get a dozen mixed and four black coffees, please? Thank you." I say to her hoping she doesn't start with the gossip.

Smiling, she replies back, "Sure hon. Will that be all?"

"Yes ma'am." I respond smiling, thinking I might actually get out without any gossip.

"Okay." She says as she starts boxing up the doughnuts. "Say, did you hear about Ricky Mack's boy?"

Here we go.

"No ma'am." I say trying to think of anything to get her to hurry up.

"Well, you know they say he on that stuff. Say someone found him behind Brock's grocery store trying to tongue kiss an alley cat. And chile let me tell you, they say the cat was not having it and tore his face all up. They said he looked like Freddy Kruger when that cat got through with him." She says laughing. "Personally, if you ask me, I think Susie Ross did it to him....."

Finally, not able to take it anymore, I tell her, "Not to interrupt, Mrs. Jenkins, but I really need to get going. Bullet is on some new meds, and it makes him have to use the bathroom a lot."

Mrs. Jenkins looks at me, then Bullet, then quickly finishes putting my order together. Yeah, the thought of Bullet's big ass shitting in her shop is enough for her to hurry up and get us out ASAP.

Gossips kill me, like every time they're telling a story they're like "they said". Who the hell is "they"? We all know "they" is really you.

After paying for my order, I thank Mrs. Jenkins. As I turn to leave, a tall, handsome black man steps inside. He had to be at least 6'4" with dark brown skin, a short tapered fro, and dressed very well. His eyes were the lightest brown I had ever seen, but something was off about him.

His smell wasn't right. It had my wolf in defensive mode. Even Bullet started to growl.

"Let's go boy." I say to Bullet while tugging on his leash. "Excuse me." I say to the guy because he's blocking the door. He's just standing there staring.

I'm starting to get a little creeped out. He's looking at me like he knows me and for some eerie feeling I think I know him too. Finally, he moves to the side letting us out, but not before taking in a deep breath. *Weird.*

After leaving out of the donut shop, I get Bullet settled in my truck, we're on our way to the shop. As I'm pulling up on the block, I'm almost cut off by three motorcycles. I lay on my horn and yell, "Watch it, mutha fucka's!!!"

The one in the front turns his head, looks at me with these weird-ass grey eyes, then proceeds to flip me off then has the nerve to blow me a kiss.

Cocky fucka.

I take a good look at the leather vests that they have on. No secret they're part of some motorcycle club. There's a big deranged looking wolf on the back with red eyes and blood hanging from its fangs. Devil Wolves is stitched on the top. Something about those eyes made my stomach flutter but I brush it off. It's not uncommon to see motorcycle clubs in the area. They speed on down the street like they didn't just cut me off. What a way to start the morning, not.

I park in front of Sultry Ink and jump out. I see Hoss is already here. Stepping to the back, I let Bullet out and head inside.

"Why you keep bringing that big ass horse up here?" Hoss asks looking up from tattooing his client.

"First of all, he's not a horse. You must have missed the part on learning your animals when you were younger and second because he's mine and he's family! I let your ass in here... don't I? Don't listen to him Bullet, you know he's a hater", I say while stroking his head. "Little pussy", I say under my breath.

Hoss now with a serious look on his face replies, "I heard that! Anyway, that big mutha fucka be knocking shit over and be up in here farting and shit. Last week my client stopped her session and rescheduled because she thought it was me!! Nasty ass, and if he chews on my cords again, I'm fucking him up!"

"Hoss please, you not going to do shit. You not slick, you don't think nobody hear you baby talking to his big ass when you in the back, *"Heyyyy Bullet, who's a good boy huh, who's a good boy?'* Boy, please. I know all about that bag of doggie treats you keep in that middle drawer too. Plus, it probably was your stanking ass farting up in here trying to blame it on my dog, fuck outta here," I say laughing out loud.

"Whatever. Those treats are for Rocket's eagle heads", he replies laughing.

Laughing at his crazy ass, I say, "Damn that's cold."

"What's cold?" Rocket asks while coming in from the back.

Still laughing, I say, "Hoss will tell you, I got to go to my office to look over the books. Come on, Bullet."

I head to my office and take a seat at my desk. Bullet sits in his corner that has all his shit there. Food, water and a big cow bone. Booting up my computer, I look over my schedule for the day. Only three clients today and one consult. Two small tats and one that'll take about three hours to do. So, if I'm lucky I might get out early today, if there are no walk in's. Hopefully the boys can handle those.

"Hey Blu, your consult's here," Pix says while coming in and going over to hug Bullet. "See... he's family."

"Thanks Pix, can you take them to my room and get them set up for me?" I ask her while finishing up the books.

"Sure. No problem. Later Bullet," she says on her way out.

Done with the books and checking over my emails, I head to my room. Walking in, I see my consult is a young, cute blonde girl dressed like she's going to the rodeo. The guy that's with her I assume is her father looks like Sheriff Dillon from Gunsmoke, with the ten-gallon hat and boots.

"Hi, I'm Blu. Melissa, right?' I say extending my hand to shake hers.

"That's me," she says with an eager smile and deep southern drawl. "This is my boyfriend, Jake.

I hope you don't mind that I brought him along for my consult. He's here to help with some ideas."

Boyfriend, I think to myself. Wow, this girl couldn't be more than nineteen, and he looks about fifty. Damn.

"No, it's cool, he can be here," I say still in disbelief. "So, what are you looking to get?"

Melissa smiles while patting the top of her vagina. "Well, Jake thinks that I should get his picture tattooed right here."

"Really?" I ask trying not to frown or laugh.

"Hell yeah, I think it's gonna be downright smoking," Jake says while smiling hard.

Guys... no lie, I couldn't stop staring. The man is grinning so hard, like he didn't have damn near every other tooth missing. And his teeth were so brown that they looked like he just finished eating a shit sandwich. Wow, is all I can say. Turning back to Melissa, I ask her, "So, is this something you want, Melissa because once it's Done, it's permanent, and if you change your mind, removal can be costly and very painful." I tell her so she can think really hard about getting it.

"Yeah, she wants it, what the hell! Are you trying to change her mind or something?" Jake yells just a little too loud for my comfort.

Counting to ten, I turn to Jake and calmly say, "I believe my consult is with Melissa, Jake, not you. Now, I have no problem with you being here but another outburst like that and you will be asked to leave."

As Jake gets ready to reply, Rocket comes thru the door, which quickly gets Melissa's attention. Yeah… bet she's rethinking getting Uncle Festus on her nether region now.

"Everything okay in here, Blu?" Rocket asks while looking over at Jake.

Shaking my head, I say, "Yeah everything is good, just a misunderstanding."

"There was no misunderstanding, this spook is trying to talk my girl out of getting my face tattooed on her pussy!!!" Jake yells with spit flying between the picket fence he calls teeth.

"Oh my God, he didn't mean that." Melissa says looking embarrassed and turning beet red, looking between me and Rocket.

"Shut up, Melissa. Look bitch, I told you what she's getting, and you're going to do it." Jake states like he's running shit.

Bullet takes a couple of steps towards Jake, but I raise my hand to stop him. Look guys, I'm born and raised in Texas, so I know all about racism. This shit don't bother me one bit. Seems to me Jake just needs to be taught some manners is all.

"Okay, so this is how this is gonna go. Sorry Melissa, I will not be able to do your tattoo, not because I don't want to but because I think you will regret it later on down the line. Second, Jake, if you ever speak to me like that again, I will break bones on your body. Now, you can politely get the fuck out." I say standing crossing my arms over my chest and smiling at Jake.

"Nig....", before he could get the nasty word out of his chicklet mouth, I have him pinned up against the wall, feet dangling.

"Now Jake, I told you what would happen if you spoke to me like that again… didn't I? I guess you thought little old me didn't have it in me, oh but let me tell you… I do." I say to him while with my other hand grabbing his right wrist and snapping it. I let him go, and he falls to the ground screaming like a damn baby. Stooping down to his level, I tell to him,

"Look at me Jake," while my eyes begin to change to blue.

Jake gulps in air trying to breath. *Awww shit, is that piss I smell? Damn, not in my room.*

"What the hell are you?" Jake asks with a low shaky voice.

"Well Jake, my boy, I'm just your average, young, successful black woman who has made her way in this world and who will not be disrespected by a dick like you. Now get your pissy ass up and get the fuck out of my shop. If I see you around here again, I'll break more than your wrist next time." I say while letting my fangs descend and giving Jake a toothy smile.

"Jesus Christ, don't kill me, don't kill me. Come on Melissa, let's go." Jake says getting up on wobbly legs, holding his wrist, while backing towards the door. Melissa goes to him and as they leave out of the door, she turns around and gives Rocket a sexy smile.

Laughing, Rocket says, "Well… that was interesting."

I reply laughing, "Just another day in the wonderful life of Blu."

Chapter 3

The rest of the day wasn't too bad, besides one of Rocket's groupies coming in and acting a damn fool again, who Pix professionally cussed out, then threw out like yesterday's trash. I'm just finishing up my last client, when I hear front the door open. I immediately stop tattooing my client because this smell comes across my nose. It's enough to get my wolf to stir also. What the hell is that? My breathing turns heavy, and I start to shake. I feel my wolf trying to take over, and we are in a battle. I can't let my client see me change.

"Hoss!! Hoss!!" I scream out in a damn near strangled voice.

"Blu, are you okay?" my client asks sounding scared. I don't answer or look up at him because I know my eyes have changed.

"What's...." is all Hoss can get out when he notices my shaking body and my eyes.

Turning to my now freaked out client, Hoss tells him, "Bro, I'm sorry, but Blu's going to have to finish your tattoo at another time. Go see Pix, and she'll reschedule you for later this week."

"But it's almost done. I've been in here for the last three hours," my client whines.

"Bro, do what the fuck I just told you!!" Hoss yells, making the client jump up and run for the door.

Hoss, now at my side, asks, "Blu, what the fuck is wrong with you?"

"I... I don't know. I was tatting, this smell came across my nose, and now I'm battling my wolf hard. She's trying to come out." I tell him as my voice sounds heavier than normal.

"Well damn," comes from a thick, sexy voice at the door. I look up, and it's the same cocky mutha fucka that was on the motorcycle that flipped me off then blew me a damn kiss.

"Who the fuck are you, and why are you up in here?" Hoss asks with a snarl. I can tell he's in protective big brother mode.

Smirking at Hoss, the sexy intruder says, "Down big boy, I'm Jax. My brothers and I came in to get tatted. I heard the commotion but smelled her first."

"What the fuck you mean you smelled her first?" Hoss asks then realizing the answer. "Ahh shit, you're a wolf too."

"Why yes I am, pussy cat," Jax says to Hoss but looking at me. I can't take my eyes off of him. He's got to be 6'4" maybe 5", built like a freight train, tanned skin from riding in the sun too long with a mustache connected to a long beard, and long brown hair that he has pulled back in a ponytail.

"I got your pussy cat, mutha fucka! You need to stop staring at my sister and get the fuck out of here!!" Hoss says while standing, cracking his neck.

"Can't do that, *Brother,*" Jax says with a smirk on his face.

"This mutha fucka looking to get his ass dragged up in here. And why the fuck not, bitch?"

Jax answers smiling at me with his fangs showing. "Because she is my mate." *Damn, did he just drop the mic?*

Okay, look you, I know all about this mate shit. My dad explained it to me after my first shift at fifteen. Every wolf has their one true mate. The bond between the two is so powerful it's like bringing two halves together, making them whole. In order for the bond to be sealed, they must bite each other during a full moon while in the heat of passion. If they are away from each other for too long, both will start to feel a pain so deep it feels like they are dying. Now, one can deny the mating bond, but they will continue to feel the pull of the other. They can be with other's but will always feel for their mate, their other missing half.

Now, do I believe in true mates? Yes because of what my parents went through, but did I ever think I would find mines? HELL NO!!! After seeing what the effects of losing a mate did to my father, I swore I would never go through that. He tried to hide his pain and loneliness from me, but I knew. I never wanted to feel a bond that strong only to have it taken away from me.

This cannot be happening!! I'm 26 years old. I've met male shifters, hell even humans and never felt this type of pull. My skin feels like it's on fire. I'm sweating like someone's pouring water all over me. My stomach feels like I am having the worst cramps in my life and my pussy is pulsing like a heartbeat. It's like this Jax has somehow started my heat, and unfortunately the only way to relieve me of all this is to fuck him. Damn, He needs to go, now, but my wolf is fighting to get out to him.

In a shaky voice looking Jax dead in his eyes I say, "You need to leave."

I'm fighting this hard because all I really want to do is kick Hoss the fuck out and let Jax take the pain away, but I don't know this man from Adam. He shows up and claims he's my true mate. Yeah, I know he is, but I don't have to accept the bond. Right?

"Dog, you heard her. You need to get the fuck on." Hoss says while pointing to the door.

"As I said before, I can't do that. You know what it means when you find your true mate, or do you pussies do it differently," the cocky fucker says.

Stepping into Jax's personal space, talons starting to descend, Hoss hisses, "It's the same mutt," Oh shit, it's like looking at two titans about to throw down.

"Then, you know what she is going through right now and the only one to ease her through this is me, her true mate, not you, *brother*." Jax says while closing the small distance between them so now they are damn near touching noses.

"Ssstop, both of you," I say shaking. "Hoss, just take me home. Jax, I don't know you and even if you are my true mate, that doesn't mean I have to accept the bond." I say while trying to stand at the same time Pix, Rocket, and two other big ass bikers come barreling into the room.

"What the fuck, Jax," the biker with the flaming red hair and five o'clock shadow says while looking at me with nostrils flaring. Damn, he's a wolf too. I know he can smell my pheromones on overdrive.

Jax says damn near growling. "It seems my mate has gone into heat, Steady."

"The fuck you mean, mate? Heat?" says the blonde damn near panting, slowly moving closer to me. Wolf too, damn.

"Get the fuck back, Deadwood, unless you ready to die tonight," Jax growls out, eyes now so grey they look white. This crazy wolf has some serious Alpha dominance radiating off him.

Looking at Jax, Deadwood says, "No disrespect, Prez, but this bitch is letting off some serious fuck me fumes."

"Call my sister a bitch again, and I will personally kill your dirty looking ass," Hoss says stepping to Deadwood.

Smirking at Hoss, Deadwood replies, "Like I said, no disrespect, *brother*."Pix asks in her calm but shaky voice. "Blu, are you okay?" I shake my head no.

"Pix take Blu and Bullet home. Take her truck and stay with her till Hoss and I get there. I don't want these fuckers following you." Rocket tells Pix, now standing next to Hoss.

Pix nods in agreement and helps me stand. As we make our way to the door, there is shouting, and I am pulled into a hard body that I know is Jax. It happened so fast that he didn't see that I had pulled my gun from the back of my shirt and had it under his chin.

With a shit eating grin on his face, he sniffs me and whispers in my ear, "I'll see you soon, Baby girl. You and I both know I am the only one to fuck the pain away."

I snatch away from him with my gun still trained on him as he's smiling, giving me the look of a predator stalking his prey. *Damn, I'm screwed.*

Chapter 4

After Pix got me home, she helped me get into a hot bath, which kind of helped some. Hoss and Rocket showed up a few hours later explaining that it took a little physical persuasion to get Jax and his crew to finally leave.

Looking concerned, Hoss asks, "Blu, what are you gonna do?"

"I don't know, Bro. I just need to rest right now and worry about Jax later. You guys can go. I'm feeling better, since I'm not so close to him now." I say while adjusting myself in my bed.

Hoss gives me a worried look, but then says, "Okay Sis, I know you can handle yourself. But if anything, and I mean anything pops off, you better call me. I'll take Bullet with me because I don't want him fucking up your rest with his big horse ass."

Laughing I tell him, "But you love him though."

Shaking his head and smiling, he gives me a kiss on the forehead leaving out of the room. Pix and Rocket came in to say their goodbyes. It took another 10 minutes to convince Pix that I would be fine before Hoss came back and carried her ass out screaming, she'll call me in the morning.

I wake up sweating, shaking and in pain again. He's here I can feel him. My body is reacting the same way as before. How did he find my home? Hoss said they weren't followed. *Fucking wolf senses.*

Jax starts pounding on my front door and yelling, "Blu, I know you're in there, come open the door!" *What the hell?*

"I can smell you, Blu. I can feel the pull, and I know you do too." He says sounding exasperated.

I sure as shit can.

Still pounding, he continues, "You think you are the only one suffering here? I told your brother that I wouldn't come, but the pull was too strong to fight it. I tried, but my wolf wants his mate and so do I!! So, why don't you put all of us out of misery and come open the fucking door Baby girl."

I'm thinking it's either Fight or flight. Hell, we all know if I open that door there will be no fight. I'll let him mount me like the bitch in heat I am. So, it's flight. Descending down the stairs as quietly as I can, I make my way to the back door. Quietly opening it, I tiptoe out and take about five steps before I hear,

"Going somewhere, Baby girl?" Jax asks breathing hard and smirking.

Damn busted.

"Don't run, darlin'. It'll only make my wolf want you more." He says with a shit eating grin on his face. *Cocky fucker. Well fuck him, his wolf, and stupid ass heat,* I think as I take off running towards the forest to the right of my house.

Zigzagging between the trees, I hear him behind me, but this fucker has let his wolf out. This wolf has got to be this biggest wolf I've ever seen in my life. My dad's wolf stood almost six feet. Jax's wolf has to be damn near seven to eight. His fur is all black which in contrast to those freaky greyish white eyes is sexy and scary as hell. My horny ass wolf is fighting me to let her out. If I do, she'll submit to his ass. So, I keep running trying to lose him in the process. I know he's playing with me. He'll get close enough to swipe my heels or nip at my ankles. Making a sharp turn to the left, I run into a thicket of bushes. Having had enough of trying to out run him on two legs, I finally let my wolf free. As I've gotten older, the change doesn't hurt like it used to. It's just second nature now, like taking off your clothes. Just when I think I've made some distance between us, I'm toppled to the ground by his wolf. I'm struggling to get him off me. I swipe my paw towards his face, only to land on my back and penned down. I look up and those grey almost white eyes are staring right back at me. I start to fight again, but he lets out a loud growl and bites down on my neck instantly stilling my movements. *Fucking Alpha.*

Nuzzling me where he bit me, his snout begins to flare. I can feel the pull of the bond so strong, but I continue to fight it. Jax shifts back into his human form with those damn eyes still on me. He rubs his face in my fur and nuzzles my neck.

Caressing my face, Jax says, "You are such a beautiful wolf, Blu. I've never seen a wolf with fur that looks like the purest snow. I can see where you get your name. Eyes so blue they look like I'm looking in the bluest ocean."

Fuck, why must he say such things? My heart starts to flutter faster. It's got to be the pull of the bond. I let out a growl and start to struggle to get away from him again.

"Submit now, Blu! Change back now!" Jax shouts throwing off enough dominance that has me shifting back to my human form. *Fucking Alpha.*

"Why are you fighting this, Baby girl, you know this is our way? I know you don't know me, but you will, starting with my cock inside you. And as I'm tearing *MY* pussy up, you will know who you belong to. I'm going to have you screaming my name so many times you won't be able to talk tomorrow." He says while lowering his hand to my pussy that's slick with my essence. He runs his fingers over my opening, and I can't help the little moan that escapes my mouth, "You wet for me, Baby girl, huh? You can fight it, but your body doesn't lie." He says as he brings his fingers to his mouth and licks them clean. "Hmmm, like the sweetest ambrosia I've ever tasted. I will claim you at the next full moon sealing our bond completely."

Damn, I'm screwed. Jax begins to massage my breasts, pinching my nipples while kissing my neck, damn if the shit doesn't feel good. He slides his left hand down my stomach and back to my pussy where he starts to play with my clit.

"Open for me, Baby girl."

It's like my legs have a mind of their own because they fall all the way open.

"Good girl."

Jax says while inserting a finger in. The shit feels so good, I'm starting to pant, must be the heat. Jax moves his head to my breasts, suckling on them both as he slowly kisses his way down to my pussy, he's still playing in. He stops, then brings his nose to my pussy and inhales deeply before saying, "Mine," then taking a long swipe of my pussy with his wolf tongue. My eyes roll in the back of my head.

It's so intense. He is licking my clit with such intensity that I'm about to cum. Jax inserts another finger and begins to fuck me in the same rhythm as his tongue.

"You like that, darlin'?" he asks against my clit.

I'm in such a state of euphoria I can't even respond back. I guess not answering wasn't a good thing because now he has latched onto my clit again and is sucking on it harder and finger fucking my pussy so fast that I am cumming harder than I ever have in my life. My back has bowed off the ground. There is a burst of stars behind my eyelids and Jax doesn't let up. I am squirting so much his face looks like damn glazed doughnut. As my orgasm starts to ebb, Jax remove his fingers and kisses his way back up my body. When he gets face to face with me, I pull him down to me and crash my mouth to his. I taste my own sweet essence on his lips. *Sexy.* As we kiss like two wild people, I lower my hand between us and grab his dick. My hand can't even wrap around it, it's so thick. Now I've been with a few men before and none where ever this thick and long as Jax. I'm talking at least eleven inches. How the hell is this anaconda going fit in me? I begin to stroke him from the base all the way up to his mushroom head.

He is literally going to tear my pussy up, I think to myself as I stop stoking the third leg he calls a dick.

"Don't be afraid", Jax says in soothing voice. "I am your true mate. I was made for you as you were made for me. I'll fit. Now put me in Babygirl."

As I look in his eyes, I can see the truth in them. He was made for me. I slowly bring the head of his cock to my opening and run it between my slit.

Jax hisses and says, "Damn, quit playing darlin' and put me in."

I slide his head back to opening and in one swift motion Jax is buried balls deep in me. We both let out loud moans. "Mine," he says. "So good, so tight."

He kisses me all over my face, giving me enough time to adjust to his size. After a few seconds, he starts to move slowly in and out of my pussy. It feels so good I begin to move with him.

"Jax," I moan.

"That's right, darling, the only man's name you will ever call out. This is my pussy," he says while pounding my pussy harder. "Who does this pussy belong to, Blu?" He asks as he now starts rubbing my clit. "Who does this pussy belong to, Blu?' He asks again as he continues his assault on my pussy.

Damn, this man has me ready to tell him it's his from the way he has my body feeling so good right now. I'm almost there. I can feel the tingle start from the tip of my toes and work its way up. I'm so wet and gushy now I'm leaking on ground.

As he says, "I asked whose does this pussy belong to Blu?"

He pinches my clit, fucking me relentless. I explode screaming his name, cumming on his dick, and squirting all over his stomach. Squeezing my eyes shut, I can feel my wolf trying to break through again. I know my eyes have changed. I fight her to stay in control.

"Open your eyes, Blu!" Jax snarls at me.

I can see that his eyes have changed too, and his wolf is close.

"You are mine. Our bond will be sealed. I will claim you. I will never let you go", he whispers to me as I feel his cock grow even larger while he's still fucking me.

He throws his head back and lets out loud howl as he cums deep inside me triggering another earth shattering orgasm out of me. I scream his name as everything goes black.

Chapter 5

I awake the next morning in my bed, with the pain from the day before gone. Maybe it was a dream, but I know it wasn't because I can still smell Jax's scent on me, as well as the minor soreness between my legs. As I'm replaying what happened between me and Jax last night, my bathroom door opens. Jax walks out with only a towel wrapped around his waist and another he's using to dry his hair. Damn he has a body of a God. I give him an appraising look from head to toe, the man has toned muscular legs and abs so defined they looked painted on. Arms so thick they look like they could crush a head in a headlock, and he's covered in tattoos. Talk about walking sexiness.

"Morning, Baby girl." He says in that sexy fuck me voice that has me wanting him again.

Damn heat.

Pushing past the urge to knock his big ass down and fuck him, I calmly ask, "Why are you still here?"

With that shit eating grin on his face again, he replies, "You know why I'm still here, darling."

"We fucked, that's it. Nothing more. Nothing less. Yeah, it was good, but I cannot be your mate." I tell him while getting out of the bed and walking towards to the bathroom.

Jax grabs me by the waist and pulls me hard against his still wet body. "Too late for that, darling. I told you, you belong to me now, and I'm never letting you go. You even confirmed it last night by screaming out my name while cumming on my dick." The cocky fucker says in my ear.

Lord, why do I just want to wrap my legs around him and let him fuck me back to sleep.

Fucking heat.

Jax's hand goes to my pussy, that's slick with my essence, and starts rubbing between my slit.

"This right here lets me know you are mine. You feel that, Baby girl, you feel how wet you are for me, how your body is calling out for me, how your wolf is calling out to mine? Well guess what? Your heat is over. This is all you and your wolf wanting me and mine's. Don't fight us, babe, because we're going to win." He says while flicking my clit and inserting a finger.

I start moaning and fucking his finger like it's his dick as he adds another finger fucking me faster. I have to wrap my arms around his neck for leverage.

"That's right, darling, cum for your mate. Cum on my fingers, Baby girl," he says, making me like a river.

My knees begin to buckle as Jax catches me with his other arm keeping me from falling. Jax slowly removes his fingers. Bringing them to his mouth sucking them clean, "Ambrosia," he says looking me in the eyes.

I push away from him and head into the bathroom slamming the door in his laughing face.

Arrogant fuck.

What have I gotten myself into? Is what I think as I take a hot shower.

There is no denying I'm attracted to Jax, this whole mate thing is crazy. I always thought my parents were crazy talking about the pulling of the bond being so strong it's like an instant love. At least that's the way they described their pull. Plus, they grew up in the same pack, they knew each other. I don't know Jax. What a cluster this is. The only way I can see this whole bonding working is if we get to know each other. I need to know if it can be more than just physical between us. We need to have a serious conversation.

After I finish my shower and hygiene, I get dressed in a pair of black leggings, tank top, and my Doc's. Pulling my dreads up in a messy bun, I head out of my bedroom. On my way down the stairs, I hear Jax raising his voice to someone. I sniff the air......Hoss.

"Blu, I know your crazy ass is by the fucking stairs. You want to tell me why this mutha fucka in here cooking eggs like Ving Rhames in Babyboy?" Hoss asks with enough venom laced in his voice to give me pause before entering the kitchen.

Holding in my laugh, I enter the kitchen and sure enough, Jax is scrambling up some eggs in his birthday suit.

"What the hell, Jax, what happened to the towel you had on? You're going to get grease burns on your dick from the bacon." I say still trying not to laugh.

Giving my body a long once over then winking, Jax replies, "I had to dry my hands off."

Asshole.

I walk over to him snatching the spatula out of his hand. I beg, "Can you go put your

clothes on? Please?"

Hoss snarls at Jax. "Yeah, put them shits on and get the fuck out!"

"Chill Bro, let him go get dressed while I talk to you," I plead with Hoss while Jax leaves the kitchen.

Walking over to me mad as hell, Hoss hisses, "What the fuck, Blu? How you got this cocky mutha fucka all up in your house cooking eggs and shit like he lives here?"

Hanging my head down, I tell him, "Hoss look, I know how it looks. Well it is how it looks but you have to understand. Last night he came here after he said he told you he wouldn't, but the pull was too strong for either one of us. I tried to fight it, hell. I even ran knowing damn well that was the worst thing to do."

"Nooo? You ran, Sis?" Hoss asks frowning at me like I'm crazy or some shit.

"Hell yeah, I ran. Shit, I told you I was trying to fight this shit. But that only made it worse. He caught me and the rest kind of just happened." I shrug not meeting his eyes.

Smirking, Hoss replies, "Well damn, at least it wasn't a full moon last night, because if it was, your ass would have been claimed."

“I know right!! I'm so screwed, literally and figuratively." I say shaking my head in my hands.

Folding his arms, he asks, "So, what do you want to do? You don't have to accept the bond and be claimed. We can run Hell's Angel out town."

Hoss and I both whip our heads around when we hear Jax say while standing the doorway, "Not going happen, *brother,* and it’s Devil Wolves."

Mine, calls out my wolf in my head.

Horny heifer.

Closing the distance between him and Jax, Hoss tells him, "If Blu doesn't want to accept the damn bond then that's what’s gonna happen."

Rubbing my temples, I think, *God not again.*

"Hoss, chill." I say coming to stand between the both of them.

“Yeah Hoss, chill." Jax's cocky ass throws in with a smirk.

Frowning I say, "You chill too, Jax, damn."

He throws both hands up like he's surrendering.

Yeah right, I think.

I turn back to Hoss," Look Bro, this is all new to me. You know Dad explained the whole bonding and claiming shit to me. I know this is our kind's way. I just need you to trust me when I say I'm not going into this blind."

Then I turn to Jax, "And the same goes for you, too. Just because we have the pull of the bond does not mean I will bow down willingly to it or you. I am an Alpha too, so you will show me the same respect. Now, we can explore getting to know each other, more than just the physical, and if things work out by the next full moon, "We", I state pointing between him and I, "Will claim each other."

He replies, smirking at me, "Fair enough, but I already know the outcome."

"Cocky mutha fucka." Hoss spits, sitting at the island in the middle of the kitchen.

"I am cocky, right darling?" Jax asks looking at me wiggling his eyebrows.

"Whatever. Anyways, what's up Bro? Why you here so early and where's Bullet?" I ask while I finish making breakfast.

Taking his glare off Jax, Hoss answers, "Well, I came by to see how you were doing this morning but imagine my surprise when I saw Ghost rider's naked ass twirling a damn spatula," he points to Jax. "Bullet's out back giving pony rides to the squirrels," he laughs. "Plus, Pix called me on my way here and said some African guy came by looking for you at the shop earlier." his tone turning serious.

I drop the spatula as soon as he finishes saying that. My body instantly starts to shake. It can't be, not after all this time.

"Baby girl! Baby girl!" Jax is yelling at me, shaking me by the shoulders. "What's wrong?"

I wonder with a shaky voice. "Hoss, you don't think it's "them" do you? Oh my God, the guy at the bakery."

"What guy from the bakery?" Hoss shouts.

I hear Jax damn near growling, "Who the fuck is *them*?"

Right before everything goes black.

Shit.

Chapter 6

When I come to, I'm back lying in my bed, Pix is sitting next to me holding a cold cloth on my head.

"Hey hon, how are you feeling?" Pix questions with a look of concern.

Giving her a reassuring smile, I reply, "Okay, where's Jax and Hoss?"

"They're downstairs with Rocket, Steady, and Deadwood." She answers back, taking the cloth of my forehead.

Looking at her confused, I question her, "Why are they all here?"

"Well after that guy left, Rocket chased the guy down and asked him what he wanted with you. He told Rocket that he came here from Africa to claim what his father couldn't. That your father stole your mother away from his and brought shame to his family. He said the only way to restore his families name is if he claims you and take you back to Africa. Rocket was about to jump the guy when five other guys came out of nowhere ready to attack him. He told Rocket to tell you that he will see you soon." She finishes with worry and fear written all over her face.

Could this shit get any crazier, yesterday I find my true mate, whom I'm not sure I want, now this loon shows up talking about claiming me and taking me back to Africa. What the hell? Less than 48 hours ago I was living the perfect life, shit just got real.

"Baby girl." I hear taking me away from my thoughts.

Jax enters the bedroom coming to the other side of the bed.

Jax turns to Pix, "Hey, Pix can you give us a few minutes?"

She stands, giving me a hug, then walks out the door.

"Baby girl, Hoss told me what happened with your parents. We suspect the guy at the bakery is either the same asshole or someone who works for him. Tell me what happened at the bakery."

I begin to tell him what happened and how something about the guys smell wasn't right. It was just off.

When I finish telling him what happened he replies, "Well he's in for a world of shit if he thinks he can come in try to take what belongs to me!"

Tired of the Alpha dominance shit, I start, "I don't belong..."

"Yes, the fuck you do!" He growls out, eyes starting to change. "You know it and so do I. You can keep denying it all you want but we both know the truth. Do you honestly think now that I have found you, I'm going let you go? Hell no! You think I'm just going let you walk away from me and that fucker gets a chance to claim you. Hell no! You are my mate! My woman! The woman who I will spend the rest of my life with! The one who will bear my children! I ain't giving that up for nobody, not even you." He snarls at me before claiming my mouth with the most passionate kiss.

I moan into his mouth. I know the human part of me is saying it's too soon, but my true being, my wolf nature knows I can't fight this even if I wanted to.

Jax pulls away looking at me, "That's right we belong to each other. No more fighting it, okay?"

I nod my head in agreement while laying it on his chest. "So what do we do now? Because there is no way I'm letting that man claim me or try to take me back to Africa."

"Not going to happen, Blu. Look, the guys and I have come up with a plan. We're going to invite our little friend out here for a little chat. I'm going to nicely explain to the prick that he came all the way over here for nothing. What he's looking for does not exist. I am your mate and there is nothing he can do about it. If he doesn't take kindly to what I tell him then..."

He trails off looking like he's on the verge of changing.

Patting him on the chest, I say, "Okay I get that, but I'm sitting in on this chat."

"No, I don't want you near that fuck!" Jax hisses out.

"Well since this concerns me, and it's going be here at my house, I'm in and that's that." I snap at him with my wolf scratching at the surface. "I can take care of myself babe. My dad taught me how to defend myself and shoot. The guy doesn't know who he's fucking with." I smirk.

Smiling, he looks at me shaking his head. "You know once I claim you, you're going to have to turn your Alpha down a bit?"

While grabbing his cock, smirking at him, I purr "Yeah not going to happen, babe. Think of how fucking sexy it'll be fighting for dominance."

Closing his eyes and groaning, he grabs my hand that wrapped around his cock and gives it a hard squeeze. "Yeah darlin' real sexy", he says while bringing his lips down on mine, kissing me into submission.

Damn I want this man. Shit. I'm gone. Jax bites my bottom lip piercing it till I taste blood. He licks my lip cleaning the blood off before pulling away. Looking at me with those freaky eyes while interlocking my fingers with his, he leads me out the bedroom door.

"Come on darling let's see what else the crew has come up with."

Entering the living room, everyone turns to look at us. Hoss is standing next to my fireplace. Rocket is sitting in the recliner with Steady to the left on my sofa and oddly on the other side of the room, Pix is sitting really close next to Deadwood. Looking like a deer in headlights. I wonder what's up with that.

Walking over to me then pulling me into a hug, Hoss asks, "Sis, you good?"

"Yeah Bro I'm good. It just caught me off guard, is all. I'm good though." I promise, giving him a squeeze.

Turning to the others, "I know some of you know my history, but I feel that I must explain it to you all since you're here to help me." Taking a deep breath, I start again. "My parents were from a wolf pack in Africa and left the pack to come here to America. Long story short, they were true mates. My grandfather, who I don't know, had arranged for my mother to marry the son of an Alpha from another pack. My parents didn't want that to happen, so they left. So, I think this guy is here as a result of that. Jax told me what you guys have planned, I'm in. What else have you guys come up with?"

Shaking his head, Hoss answers, "No you not in this Blu, it's too dangerous."

"Hoss, I'll tell you like I told Jax, I'm in this. This is about me," I stress, pointing to my chest. "This stupid ass has come here threating me not you. You know this is what Dad was preparing me for. He knew this day would eventually come." I say voice cracking with emotion.

Now hugging me tighter Hoss whispers, "Sis, please."

"No, Hoss this has to end. I don't want to have to keep looking over my shoulder the rest of my life." Turning to everyone in the room, I continue, "I appreciate you all wanting to help me. My Dad told me this day might come, but he hoped it never would. Hell I hoped it never would. He trained me for this. I'm ready. So, either we're all in this together, or I do this on my own."

Taking me from Hoss' embrace Jax states, "Not a chance, Baby girl. We're all in but you better not get one fucking scratch on you, or I will kill him."

"That's fine with me," I return standing on my tip toes kissing his cheek.

Looking at everyone in the room, Hoss speaks, "All right then Sis, let's get this set up. Rocket, go back to town and tell that piece of shit to meet Blu here at seven o'clock. Tell his ass don't come any earlier and don't be late. Then bring your ass right back here, got it?" He explains while directing Rocket to the door.

"Be careful man, we don't know how this fool moves, okay," Hoss whispers to Rocket, placing his hands on his shoulders.

"I got it Bro. Be back in a bit Sis," Rocket promises to me as he leaves out the door.

Pix looking at Hoss, "So, now what do we do?"

"Blu, I think it's time to go to the fun room," Hoss suggests, looking at me with a wicked smirk plastered across his face.

Grinning like a Cheshire cat I tell him, "Yeah, I think your right."

"What's in the fun room?" Steady wonders, questionably.

"My toys," smiling hard, I answer him.

Chapter 7

"Toys? Toys? Damn Blu, I thought you were talking about whips and chains. You know some freaky type of shit." Deadwood comments, wiggling his eyebrows. "This is a fucking arsenal." He frowns, letting out a slow whistle.

On all four walls of my fun room is every type of weaponry you can think of. From Colt 45's to AR 16 rifles. On the counter to the right there are different styles and sizes of knives and on the counter on the left, is all my cleaning supplies for my weapons.

Jax asks raising his eyebrow at me. "Baby girl, why do you have all this shit?"

"This was my Dads arsenal room. He was a police detective. I told you he wanted me to always be prepared." I answer him laughing. "Plus, I kinda have an obsession for them."

"Well damn, should I be scared of you?" He questions, laughing now too.

"Hell, I am!" Deadwood exclaims, looking serious and a little scared.

"You should be," Pix mutters reaching over grabbing the Butterfly knife.

"Whoa there, little lady, you need to be careful with that," Deadwood states while trying to take the knife from her. Surprising him by stepping back, she starts twirling the knife in her hand like the pro she is. I told you all she was silent but deadly. When she finishes her hand dance with the knife, she closes it just as fast as she opened it, handing it to him. Standing there with his mouth hanging open, Deadwood takes the knife.

Turning to look at Jax laughing, Deadwood yells, "Shit! Now I'm really scared. I think I just found my true mate too, Prez."

Jax starts laughing with him, coming over to me placing his hands on the sides of my waist.

“Are you all like assassins or something babe?" He whispers in my ear.

Laughing at his craziness I reply, "No but we can fight like some. Pretty bad ass, huh?"

"Fucking sexy as hell if you ask me," He moans, pulling me closer, nuzzling his nose in my neck.

"Not now lovebirds. We got shit to handle. Grab what you need and let’s go get ready. We only got a few hours left before that asshole shows up. I already have what I need,’ Hoss says going to the door, extending his talons.

"Alright then pussy cat.", Steady purrs, smiling at Hoss.

"I got your pussy cat, mutt," Hoss throws back over his shoulder at him.

We all laugh, as Pix and Steady pick their weapons of choice.

Curious to what Jax and Deadwood will pick, I ask, "Aren't you two getting anything?"

"No darlin’. Like your brother we got all the weapons we need right here." Holding up his hand showing his large claws.

Fanning myself, I groan, "Shittttt now I'm scared."

This man gets me all types of hot, but I know now is not the time for that. Soon we'll handle that.

Jax laughs whispering in my ear while pulling me out the door, "Later Baby girl, later."

Going back into the living room, I see that Rocket has returned looking pissed.

"What happened, Rocket?" I ask with concern.

"I told that mutha fucka what the plan was and he started talking reckless. Talking about you belong to him because the arrangement that your grandfathers had in place for his father and your mother was not obligated so now it defaults to you. He said he's coming, and he's not leaving without you."

Jax lets out a growl and hisses between his teeth, "Did you tell him about me?"

"No." Rocket replies, smiling at him. "I wanted you to be a surprise."

"Damn straight, I'm his fucking surprise," Jax grunts out with everyone laughing.

Chapter 8

As the guys are in the back yard going over the plan, Pix and I are in the kitchen making sandwiches for everyone.

Curious to see what's up with her and Deadwood, I question her. "So, what's up, Pix? You and Deadwood sure looked mighty comfortable on the loveseat earlier. What's up with that?" I tease her giving a questioning look.

"I don't know what you're talking about. We just so happen to sit on the same couch, no big deal." She answers looking like she just got caught with her had in the cookie jar.

Giving her a small smile, "You sure?"

"Yeah I'm sure. I mean he's hot and all. Really handsome in that rugged biker kind of way, tall like a mountain, with a body thick like a football player and did you see his eyes?" She rambles on while chopping the hell out of the tomatoes.

Shocked by her reaction, I quickly respond, "Hey, hey Pix you're supposed to slice the tomatoes, not make salsa. Damn, if I didn't know any better, I'd think you had the hots for him."

"Okay, look I think he's really hot okay. There I said it. Honestly though I think he's a little too much for me," she replies looking down at the now jacked up tomatoes.

"Girl, please. Did you not see how he looked at you after you put on your little knife show? I thought for sure he was going throw you on the floor and do you right there with all of us in the room," I laugh.

"Nooo, you don't really think he would have done that do you? Oh my God! See he's too much," she states, turning back to abusing the tomatoes.

Grabbing her arm to stop her from pureeing the tomatoes, I reassure her, "Pix relax. I'm just saying I think he's into you too. Go with the flow. I'm sure he can tell you're not like any of the loud crazy women he's used to, which probably makes him want you even more."

"You think so?" she asks with hope.

"Hell, yeah I do. I'm no expert on relationships, shit I just found my mate. But I do think some men like women who are mysterious. You know the ones like you, that keep them guessing and can handle their own," I state to her giving her a reassuring smile.

Now looking even more confused, she asks, "But he's a wolf and I'm a fox. How's that going work?"

"Girl, please. You're in the same species. Let the humans tell it, we're all dogs." I huff as we both start laughing.

Coming back in with the guys, Jax question, "What's going on in here?"

"Nothing. Just a little girl talk." I tell him.

"Mmm, hmm," he hums.

Not sure what's about to happen as I watch Deadwood walk over to Pix and offer her, "Hey Pix, do you want to take a walk with me?"

"Sssure" Pix replies looking at me as I give her a thumb's up.

"Cool. We'll be back before everything kicks off," Deadwood promises before grabbing two sandwiches, chips and bottles of water. Pix follows suit and grabs some napkins and a blanket out of the linen closet. Both leave out the back door.

"What's up with that?" Rocket looking like Hoss in big brother mode.

Handing him a sandwich, I answer, "Leave them alone. They're just hanging out."

"Yeah, okay. She better come back the same way she left is all I'm saying." He snarls taking a bite out his sandwich.

Guffawing at the expression on Rocket's face, I get out, "You've been around Hoss too long. Both of you seem to forget we are grown ass women and can handle ourselves. Don't get me wrong, we love and appreciate you and Hoss, but sometimes you guys got to take a step back. Pix is fine. You know she is not going let anything happen, that she doesn't want to happen."

Now cracking up at the expressions on his and Hoss' faces. Hoss with his eyebrows pinched and sour look on his face starts to say, "See that's that...."

Cutting him off I tell them, "Chill guys, I'm just messing with you all. Pix is good."

Taking a seat at the table, Jax adds, "She's fine. Under all that gruff, Deadwood is actually a good guy. He's been with me since I stared this club. He's a standup guy. Hell, I've never seen him cater to any female the way he just did with Pix, so that says a lot. Have you Steady?"

As if he had to think really hard about the question, Steady taps his finger on his chin while slowly shaking his head side to side and replies, "Nope. Damn, now both my boys have been bit by the fucking mate bug! What the hell?" He wonders looking like somebody stole his little red wagon. Spinning around to Hoss and Rocket, he tells them with big ass grin on his face, "Well, fella's I think when this is all over we need to hit up the nearest strip club, because I am not going to be sitting around watching this shit 24/7."

"You ain't never lied, Bro," Hoss scoffs dapping him up.

"Well we're going have to go to Shreveport or Dallas, because the strippers around here are throwed off. They got like one titty bigger than the other, jacked up ass implants. And don't get me started on their faces, damn. It's just sad," Rocket tsk shaking his head causing all of us to laugh.

Having finished eating and going over the plan once again with the guys, I take my plate and place it in the sink.

Feeling a little tired from the day I tell them, "Alright guys enjoy your meal. I'm going upstairs to relax for a bit before dude shows up."

"You want me to come with you Baby girl?" Jax questions.

Steady yells laughing. "See that's that shit right there I'm talking about."

"Shut the fuck up Steady. I can't wait till you find your mate, prick." Jax laughs at the frown now on Steady's face.

"Yeah. Whatever," Steady huffs before walking into the living room.

Laughing I turn to Jax and give him a quick peck on the lips telling him, "No babe. Stay and finish up with the guys. I'll see you in a bit."

Jax whispers softly against my lips. "Ok, darling, but you call me if you need me."

"I will babe." I promise him before heading upstairs.

Chapter 9

I must have fallen asleep because I'm awakened with light feather kisses on my face and neck. I already know who it is, so I decide to mess with him a little.

"Mmmmm, Robert," I purr out.

"Who the fuck is Robert?" Jax asks in a low growl.

Laughing at how quick his demeanor changed, I reply, "Nobody babe, I swear. I was just messing with you." Still laughing at the mean mugging face he has on.

"Don't play with me Blu. You're going to have me out here fucking up every prick with the name Robert."

I say rubbing my cheek on his. "For real Jax I was just playing."

"Yeah, okay. I was waking you up to let you know it go time. The asshole should be here within the next half hour." Jax states while holding me close.

"Okay. I'm ready." I tell him, while getting up and putting my boots back on.

"I'm not playing Blu, you better come out of this without a scratch on you or he will die." He says sternly.

"I will babe and the same goes for you. We walk in this together, we walk out together. Deal?"

"Deal," He states before kissing me.

As we walk into the living room Rocket informs us, "They're pulling up in the yard. Mutha fucka has no concept of time. He's like fifteen minutes early. Oh, well might as well get this shit over with."

Going to the window I see two black SUV's pull into front of the house. Three guys get out of the first SUV, followed by three in the second. Looking closely, I recognize the guy from the bakery. He's one of the guys getting out of the second SUV. As he makes his way to the front of the house, the other guys surround him like he's Obama or El Chapo. Really, who the hell is this guy?

Like he heard me ask the question out loud, the mystery man yells, "I am Yusef Okoye, exiled Prince of the Okoye Pack in South Africa. I am here to claim Blu Andora, princess of the Adeyemi Pack of South Africa." He states sternly in a deep African accent.

"No, this cocky mutha fucka didn't," Hoss hisses while going for the door.

"Hoss, wait," I call out to him. "Let me step out and talk to him."

Jax warns, "Hell no, Blue."

I plead with everyone. "Look just let me go out there and try to reason with him, okay? Let me explain to him that I am not his mate and him trying to claim me will not change the fact that my parents were true mates and had to leave the pack. Please let me do this."

"Fine but we're going out there with you. We don't know what this asshole has up his sleeve," Jax comments.

I quietly agree and reply, "Okay, let's go."

As we all step out on the front porch, I can feel Yusef's eyes burning a hole in me. Jax growls low to the side of me. Not wanting to drag this out I step forward.

"I am Blu Andora. I am not a princess of any pack in South Africa. My parents had long left the pack before I was born. They were true mates. My mother tried to explain this to her father, but he wouldn't listen. Your father was not my mother's mate, just like I am not yours. I'm sorry you came all this way for nothing, but I would never let you claim me, nor would I go back to Africa with you." I tell Yusef while staring him straight in the eyes.

Venom laced in his voice, he responds, "Oh but you are so wrong princess. My family was exiled because of your whore of a mother. She was supposed to be mated to my father. To unify the packs but then she broke the arrangement and ran away with your bastard father. My family was the laughing- stock of all surrounding packs. My father was never the same. Do you know what is like have your mate taken by a lesser wolf, Princess? Well I do. I watched my father damn near kill his self, trying to redeem our family's name. Now I'm here to rectify that. The elders have advised me that my family can be restored if I found and claimed you as my mate. Then bring you back with me. You know, correcting a wrong that happened so many years ago."

Everyone on the porch take a step closer as well as Yusef's men. I can hear the growls and feel the tension rolling off of everyone but hold my hands up to stop them.

Stepping off the porch, I shake my head in disbelief of how crazy this fool sounds.

"First of all, Yusef, is it? If you ever talk about my parents like that again, you won't make it back to Africa, well maybe you will in a body bag. Second of all as I told you before your trip here was a wasted one. Much like my parent's story, I have found my true mate and he is not you," I reply with a smirk. Instantly I feel Jax's presence behind me.

Yusef looks between Jax and me and lets out a loud growl. Clapping his hands together Yusef remarks, "It is of no consequence, Princess. Unlike my father who was never given the opportunity, I challenge your *mate* for the claim of you."

Shocked by what he just said, I start towards him, but Jax grabs my wrist.

"I accept your challenge." Jax sneers stepping in front of me.

"Jax no, you can't do this." I say pleading with him.

"The hell I can't darlin'. I told you before I'm not losing you to anything or anyone. I just found you and if this asshole thinks he's going to claim you, he must be as crazy as his old man was," growls Jax.

Turning to Yusef, Jax says, "Like I said I accept your challenge and once I have beat your ass, you and your fuck crew will leave, never to come around here again. Am I clear, *prince*?" Jax asks him while taking off his shirt, only to get a smirk back for Yusef.

Pix comes and pulls me off to the side while Hoss, Rocket, Steady, Deadwood and Yusef's men make a large circle around Jax and Yusef.

Yusef pulls off his shirt and I must say the man is definitely built. Flexing his muscles and rolling his shoulders, you can see the definition in each muscle. I turn to look at Jax. Yusef may be built but he has nothing on my mate. Almost evenly matched in height and width, Jax has him by a couple of inches.

Yusef taunts Jax, "After I beat you, white man, I will claim Blu at the next Full Moon in a couple of days. She will be mine. You shouldn't even be here."

"Well son, let me tell you, I'm where I'm supposed to be. Unlike you, I'm with my true mate. I do not have to try and force an unwanted claim on anyone. I guess like father, like son, huh?" Jax smirks.

Yusef growls as he changes into his wolf lunging at Jax. Jax steps to the right avoiding being clawed in the face. He counters and catches Yusef with a jab to the ribs. Yusef howls out and retreats. His guys try to intervene, but he stops them. Taking in deep breaths he attacks Jax again. This time Jax transforms into his wolf. They look like to wild beasts going at each other.

Yusef gets the upper hand and starts clawing at Jax's stomach. I start towards them but quickly stopped by Hoss.

"Stay. The. Fuck. Back. Blu!" Hoss growls out, voice straining with every word. I can tell he's fighting to keep his panther at bay.

Jax, now with a bloody nose and cut above his left eyebrow, turns his body to where he can latch onto Yusef's hind leg. He flips him over which gives him enough time to recover. One of Yusef's men comes from behind, sucker punching Jax in the back of the head. All hell break's loose then. Hoss ~~is~~ unable to contain his panther anymore,-shifts and charges towards the coward. Steady and Deadwood now in their wolf forms attack Yusef's men while Rocket is going toe to toe with the other.

Trying to get out of Pix's hold I yell at her, "Let me go Pix!"

"No, Blu! They can handle it," she says still holding on to me.

"They're fighting dirty!" I shout to her.

"I know, but they will handle it. Please Blu just let them take care of it," she warns with worry in her voice. All of a sudden there's a loud pop, followed by a low growl.

Turning back to brawl, we see that one of Yusef's men has shot Deadwood in his front leg. Letting out a piercing shriek, Pix instantly changes into her fox and attacks the guy. My girl is fucking him up. She's too fast for him get any kind of grip on her. I run over and check on Deadwood, who has shifted back into his human form.

"Oh my God, are you hurt bad?" I ask looking at his leg that's bleeding pretty good now.

Wincing he replies, "No, it's just a flesh wound. What the fuck is Pix doing? Go get her! If that mutha fucka hurts her, he'll meet his maker today!"

"Don't worry about Pix. She can take care of herself. There are a lot of things you don't know about her, but that's her story to tell." I relay to him, ripping fabric from my shirt to wrap around his leg.

"Oh, she's definitely going to tell me," he spits with a scowl on his face. Any other time it might have been funny, but now was not it.

After wrapping up Deadwood's leg, I check to see what's going on. One of Yusef's men is down not moving. Hoss, Rocket and Steady got the upper hand with the other three, while Pix's ass is literally sitting on top of the guy who shot Deadwood, licking her paws. I told you guys my girl was silent but deadly.

Jax and Yusef are still going at it. Jax surprises Yusef with a hard hit to the face. Yusef lets out a grunt and falls to the ground. As Jax is about to strike again, Yusef quickly transforms back in to in human form. Grabbing his shredded pants, he pulls out a knife catching Jax in the side.

"Jax!" I yell as I watch my mate fall to the ground.

Slowly standing up, Yusef taunts Jax. "See white man, I told you I was going to beat you and claim *my* mate. I will not be like my father. I will unite the packs as it should have been done all those years ago." Now standing over Jax, raising the knife to end my mate's life.

As Yusef brings the knife down to kill Jax, his arm is halted. Pain instantly travels up his arm. Latched on to him are the teeth of my white wolf. He screams and struggles to shake his arm free from the clutches my wolf, only to have her rip it off. He howls out in pain. Spitting the arm out she stalks him like a predator does its prey.

"Beautiful." Yusef murmurs, staring at her in awe as electric blue eyes stare back at him. "You were supposed to be mine! I was the one to save my family's name. So, if this is how it's going to end then I might as well take you with me." Grabbing the knife again with his good hand he launches towards my white wolf. Before he can raise the knife, the she catches him by the neck with her fangs, ripping his throat out.

"Blu!" Jax screams out to me.

I turn to see Jax has changed back into his human form and is now on his back. Running over to him, I immediately start licking his face.

"Shit Blu stop," he winces out but with smile. Opening his eyes, he sees the blood around my mouth. "Even with that assholes blood on you, you're still the most beautiful wolf I've ever seen. Change back, Baby girl."

Quickly, I change back and take a look at his side.

Checking his wound, I tell him, "This will heal quicker if you shift back."

"Not until we get rid of these pricks," he growls out.

"Fine then let me help you up." I offer, helping him sit up then putting his arm around my shoulder to get him up.

"I got this Sis," Hoss promises, moving me out of the way and getting Jax to his feet. "Damn man, you heavy as shit. What the fuck you be eating?" he jokes ~~laughing~~ chuckling, then immediately stops and frowns. "Never mind, don't answer that."

Jax wince and laugh at the same time.

Surveying the area, I see Rocket and Steady are tying up Yusef's remaining men.

"Untie them, Rocket." I command, walking over to where they are at.

"What?" he asks in disbelief with a frown on his face.

"I said untie them." I repeat, turning to the men. "The only reason the three of you are still alive is because my brothers and sister had mercy on you. You will leave my property and never return. You will tell your elders what happened here today. That Yusef failed just like his father. You tell them that if anyone else comes for me again they will receive the same fate." I tell them ready to back up the threat. "You tell them if they come the white wolf will be waiting for their asses."

With his head bowed one of the men asks, "What about the bodies?"

"We will burn them." I reply as I walk away.

Epilogue

Tonight, is the night of the full moon. The night that Jax, my true mate, will claim me sealing our bond. He has since healed from the stab wound, he received from Yusef. I made him stay in wolf form for a whole day to ensure it healed properly, which was a feat in itself. Having his big ass whining for attention and Bullet thinking he had a new playmate was exhausting. Luckily Hoss came and took Bullet home with him.

We burned the bodies of Yusef and his men. Rocket and Steady took the ashes into my forest and buried them deep. The other three men got into to the SUV's and left. Hopefully they relayed the message I sent back to their elders. If not, I'll be ready if they decide to come at me again.

Pix took Deadwood home with her. We haven't seen nor heard from them since. I only pray that she has thrown caution to the wind and is tearing his ass up. Smirk.

Hoss, Rocket and Steady have been hitting damn near every strip club in Shreveport. Hoss said that Steady has some good drawing abilities and is considering taking him on as an apprentice.

"Blu? Where are you darlin'?"

I smile hearing my mate's voice coming from the living room.

"I'm in the kitchen, babe." I yell back to him.

Coming to stand behind me kissing my neck, Jax asks "What are you up to?"

"Nothing much, just finishing up the dishes from dinner. What's up with you?" I wonder drying my hands, turning around giving him a soft kiss on the lips.

"Mmmm. Nothing much, ready to properly claim my mate" he replies, hands palming my ass, giving my left cheek a squeeze.

Closing my eyes, I ask "Is that right? She must be one lucky lady."

"Oh, she is very fucking lucky," He teases grinding his hard cock against my stomach.

"Jax!!!!" I moan.

Nibbling on my ear, he responds "Yes, Blu?"

Pushing him away from me, "Catch me if you can, big boy," taking off out the back door.

Letting out a loud roar, Jax is quick to the chase. I swear this is like deja vu, when he first chased me into the woods. Only this time when we leave, we will be fully bonded. Changing into my wolf form, I run towards the lake. I hear Jax let out a howl behind me. He's in his wolf form now too. I know he's toying with me because he could have easily caught me by now, hell I'm not putting up much of a chase.

Stopping by the big Redwood, I turn and wait for him. I know he's close, I can smell his scent. Looking from left to right I try to see if I can make out his form through the darkness of the forest.

"Grrrrl," I hear behind me.

Turning I see the black wolf. He has to be the most beautiful beast I've ever seen. I will never get tired of looking at him, especially looking into those grey eyes. He slowly stalks toward me. I stand my ground. I swipe at his front right leg. He moves to block it. I do the same to the other, he does the same. Finally having enough, he changes back to his human form.

"Change back, Blu!" He orders with authority. There goes that Alpha dominance again.

Quickly changing back, I stare into his eyes. He steps closer to me. Grabbing my face between his hands, he says, "My mate. Mine." Then passionately kisses me.

Jax slowly lowers us to the ground with him on his back with me on his chest. I put my hands on his chest and start to rub my body against his. I can feel my pussy starting to leak all over his thighs. Jax brings his hands up kneading my breast, alternating pinching my nipples. I let out a moan, it feels so good. Breaking the kiss, I start kissing his cheeks and then his neck, making my way to his chest. I suck on his nipples giving each one a little bite. He shivers.

With labored breath Jax slurs out, "Blu, love I need to be in you now."

Positioning my pussy over his large erection, I slowly ease half of him inside of me. We both let out sigh of relief. Jax grips my hips and thrusts hard upwards, fully embedding his cock. I cry out. The pain and pleasure of having him stretch me to the limits has me wanting more. He starts moving under me. I begin to swirl my hips to meet his thrusts. Jax grabs my ass cheeks and spreads them, letting him go deeper into my pussy. I let out a loud moan.

Thrusting harder, Jax grunts out, "That's right darlin', feel your mate." He reaches between us and starts rubbing my clit with each thrust.

"Oh my God, Jax, I'm close, so close," I tell him as I begin to feel my orgasm coming on.

Jax sits up and wraps his arms around me, still thrusting into me. I wrap my arms around him too, hanging on for dear life.

"Look at the moon, Blu. Under this full moon I claim you as my true mate, Blu. Do you accept me as your true mate?" he asks with such emotion.

I look into his eyes and see that they have changed to his wolfs. His fangs have descended. I feel my own eyes change and fangs start to descend.

"Yes Jax, I accept you as my true mate." I respond as tears fall from my eyes.

Jax lets out a growl and bites the tendon between my neck and shoulder. I instantly start to cum. Eyes rolling to back of my head, all I see are stars as Jax continues pumping into me. I feel weightless.

"Blu, baby you have to bite me too for the bond to be complete." Jax says, as I feel he is close to his release. Instantly I bite him in the same place on his neck sealing our bond forever.

Jax cums. Spilling his seed deep in my womb, I collapse on top of him. We both lay there sweaty searching for our next breath.

"I love you, Baby girl. Are you okay?" Jax tells me, holding me tight.

Kissing him passionately, I answer, "I love you too, babe. And I'm on cloud nine, my true mate."

Jax hugs me tighter to him, rubbing his hands up and down my back. I lay there in his arms, thinking about everything that has happened. I smile thinking of my parents. Finally, really understanding what they went through for their love for one another. I never thought I would find my true mate. Didn't think he existed. I guess Fate has a way of bringing them to you when you least expect it because mine came straight *Outta The Blue* and knocked me on my ass.

The End

Made in United States
North Haven, CT
15 April 2022

18260248R00036